LIFE AS
A CAT

LIFE AS
A CAT

CHRIS WIDDOP

CONTENTS

LIFE AS A CAT

1

I was a very playful little kitten. I'd always wander off on my own, fighting imaginary villains and pretending I was a great warrior. I had big dreams back then. Some day, I really *was* going to be a great warrior. A *ninja*, in fact. And this was the day that I'd take my first step towards achieving those dreams.

I didn't want to start off too big, though. So, crawling through the tall grass, making sure my presence remained undetected, I stalked my first victim. It was a small green lizard who blended in with the environment.

I slowly approached, and as I moved, the grass shifted.

The lizard stopped in its tracks, looking around for any threats. Noticing nothing out of the ordinary, it continued to scurry on.

I crept forward then, my eyes never leaving

their target. When it appeared that the lizard had let its guard down, I scrunched down, ready to pounce.

"Rrrrrrrowr!"

I turned to the sound of the growl, but it was too late. A black tabby pounced out through the grass, tackling me and pinning me to the ground. The black cat grinned in amusement, his youthful blue eyes glowing. Upon realizing who my attacker was, I shook the shock from my face and scowled.

"Charlie!"

"Got ya again, Velcro," Charlie laughed. "You're gonna have to do better than that, sis."

I shoved my brother off of me, huffing as I sat up. But when I looked over, Charlie was no longer there. And as I looked down, I saw that I was no longer a kitten, but a cat fully grown.

I must have been dreaming again.

I wasn't sure why I was having these dreams. They felt so vivid, so real, almost like they were actually happening, like I was reliving memories from my old life. And yet the strange thing about them was that these memories didn't always play out how I remembered them. Certain details would be wrong, and it was usually when I noticed these off details that I would realize that I was merely dreaming again.

I was no longer a cat living on the physical realm. And yet, I wasn't so sure that I was dead either. But in my past life, I had indeed succeeded in becoming a ninja, and a great warrior. The last thing I recall from that life was taking down an evil Fox Spirit who had threatened the world. And after that, I slipped into this new realm, where I felt almost like a ghost, unable to interact with the world around me as I floated around in an endless limbo where I was left to ponder over the meaning of it all.

I wasn't able to ponder for too long though before my thoughts were interrupted by what sounded like some sort of yipping. It was as if something was crying out to me, like some sort of distress signal, and I couldn't help but feel compelled to follow after the call.

So I slipped past the terrain, floating over the deserts and meadows and forests and oceans with ease as I pursued the call. But as my journey brought me across a familiar rocky terrain, I found myself confronted yet again by my brother Charlie, who came sprinting my way with a sword in hand.

Suddenly I was back on the ground, sprinting his way with my own sword drawn, and our blades clashed.

"Come on and fight me," I roared, taking

another swing at him. "Show me what you *got!*"

As we parried, for a minute it appeared as if the two of us were evenly matched. But soon Charlie gained the upper hand. He succeeded in disarming me, and he held his sword pointed out in my direction.

"You're full of crap, you know that?" Charlie proclaimed. "All this time we've been doing nothing but fighting. But..." he then paused, as he sheathed his sword and held a hand out to me. "But how can we do our part to help make the world a better place if we can't even mend things and find peace between the two of us?"

"Huh?"

Then in the blink of an eye, Charlie was gone again.

I certainly recalled a moment like this from my life. But again, the details were all wrong, and in this instance, our roles were reversed from how this moment had actually transpired. In reality, Charlie was the aggressor, and I was the one who managed to disarm him. And also in reality, I was the one who called him out on *his* crap, and spoke those words to him, those words that a mutual friend had once spoken to me.

"If you can't even find peace within yourself, then how can you hope to bring peace the world over?"

Being reminded of those words made me once again think back to my final moments in the physical realm. And I couldn't help but wonder, did I ever actually manage to find peace within myself, even after I had potentially saved the world from the Fox Spirit's threat?

I heard the yipping distress call again, and this time, I realized that it wasn't coming from this plane, but from somewhere up above. And as I turned my head up towards the sky, I wondered, could this be a cry from the universe calling out to me?

2

Just as I was able to slip across the world in what seemed like an instant, I had turned to face the sky, and I thrust myself upwards. I slipped up into the blue, brushed past the clouds, and continued to fly higher and higher, until I had found myself drifting past the atmosphere and into the dark, cold immensity of space.

Onward I continued towards the yipping cry, until soon I found myself crossing past the moon. Something on the moon's surface had caught my eye though, and as I looked down, I couldn't help but feel as if something or someone was waving me down. And so I stopped, and I drifted down to the moon's surface to greet this individual.

When I arrived, I was stunned to find that it was a massive spider that had waved me over. And upon further inspection, I believed that I recognized this particular spider.

"Are you who I think you are?" I asked.

"It is indeed I, yes," the spider responded.

I narrowed my eyes. This wasn't just any spider, this was *the* Spider, a villain with whom I had fought in my past life as a ninja. But he looked different now. When we battled, he had covered most of his body in robotic mechanizations which he used to enhance his natural abilities. But as he stood before me now, he looked like the original organic being that always lied underneath those mechanical contraptions.

"What are you doing here?" I seethed. "And... how is it that you're able to see me?"

"Why, because I exist on the same plane as you, a place beyond physical limitations," the Spider said. "I transferred my consciousness to this realm some years ago, and I've been taking advantage of my new circumstance in order to expand my understanding."

"Understanding?" I asked. "Of what?"

"Of the universe. Of life itself. Of our place, and our purpose."

"Why would you care about any of that?" I said. "Back in your past life, all you cared about was playing God and torturing innocents, making the lives of those around you miserable."

"Ah yes, this is true," the Spider conceded. "But since slipping into this realm, I've found that the sheer vastness of space has a way of humbling one such as me. Yes, I tried to play God, but I can see now just how small I really was, and just how little impact all of my efforts made in the grand scheme. The universe is like the widest web of them all, connecting everything, and I'm but a mere speck upon such an incomprehensibly massive idea."

"So now what, you've had a sudden change of heart and I'm just supposed to accept that? Why did you wave me down here anyway?"

"Because, you've heard it too, haven't you?"

"You mean you heard the call as well?" I asked.

"I have, yes," said the Spider.

I turned up in the direction of the yipping distress call, when someone stepped up beside me.

"Can you see it? The stars, they're calling out to you."

I looked over to see it was a much more elderly Charlie who was standing beside me, his head turned to the sky.

"You think you have what it takes to meet this next challenge, Velcro?" he asked, then looked at me with a smile.

I shook my head, and the image of my brother beside me disappeared.

"What's wrong?" asked the Spider.

"It's nothing. I've just been having these weird visions, like moments from my life replaying before my eyes. But it feels like I'm dreaming, because the moments don't feel right."

"We are on a realm beyond the physical plane, and as such, we have no need for sleep and dreaming in order to rest our bodies," explained the Spider. "What you're experiencing aren't dreams, but memories."

"They're not, though," I argued. "Because the moments are often different from how they actually played out in reality."

"Ah, but *whose* reality?" said the Spider.

"What do you mean?" I asked.

"They say that a cat has nine lives. Well, what if that were more than just a saying? What if these moments you're experiencing aren't from *your* life, but from another that you didn't know even existed?"

"Hmm," I wondered. "But if that were so, then how could I be sure which memories are the real me?"

"Why can't they all be?" the Spider suggested. "What makes one reality more real than another?"

I considered this theory, and then I asked, "You've experienced them, too, haven't you?"

"I have. And I fear that all of those lives lived might very well be in grave danger."

"What makes you say that?"

The Spider then turned up to the call in the space above us, and I looked up as well.

"I first heard that call shortly after you had arrived on this plane. And I've listened as it has grown louder, bigger, stronger. But more than hear it, I've been able to *feel* its immense power, if just ever so slightly. Whatever it is, it's growing, and fast, and I fear that it intends to suffocate the whole universe with it."

"You've seen it, in a memory, haven't you?" I asked, looking over to him.

"I have, yes."

"And so that's why you waved me over?"

"Indeed," the Spider answered.

I studied his features. He said that he had been humbled, but he looked more scared to me. Either way though, he definitely seemed different from before.

"Well what do you suggest we do about it?" I asked.

"When the universe calls out to you, you

should answer," he said. "But be careful Ninja Kat, or you'll fly too close to the sun."

3

Even within the unbelievable vastness of space, we were able to slip seamlessly through as we flew toward the distressing call. In an instant we traveled the distance between planets, between galaxies, until we reached the spot in the universe in which the call was coming from, a star in the great distance which was growing larger the closer we got.

As we continued our approach, we noticed the nearby planets were set completely aflame, a horrific sight which stopped me in my tracks and triggered an equally horrific memory from my past life. Suddenly I was standing atop a high mountain, looking down under the red sky at the world beneath me as it was being engulfed by fire. And all I could do in that moment was gawk in horror and utter under my breath, "*God.*"

"What is it?" asked the Spider, snapping me

out of my trance.

"It's just, these planets on fire, it reminds me of when the Fox Spirit set our own world on fire," I said.

"Hmm, I wonder if there's a correlation there," said the Spider. "Is whatever we're tracking down threatening to similarly set the entire universe, the whole of reality ablaze?"

"I won't let that happen," I said firmly. "I won't let whatever this is hurt my friends, or anyone else."

"I'm afraid it's very possibly already too late for that," said the Spider.

"What do you mean?"

"You mean you haven't noticed yet? Time moves differently in this realm. What feels like an instant to us in our travels could in reality be far longer than that, though how long exactly I'm afraid I can't say."

"So then you mean..." I said, the sudden realization striking me, "You mean, the universe we're trying to save now isn't even the same one we lived in before? Our world may be already gone?"

"As we know it, yes. *But*, just because our home may not be recognizable, does that alone mean that it's suddenly not still worth saving?"

The Spider was right, and I couldn't believe I was hearing these words out of him of all creatures. So I shook my worrisome thoughts from my mind, and I looked ahead once more to our destination, and to the yipping calls that continued to grow louder.

And then we were close enough to see it clearly. Though it was still light-years away from us, we could see the massive star that had threatened our universe. We watched as it expanded at a concerning rate. I noticed what at first appeared to be two solar flares swaying behind it, but which soon came to more resemble two whipping tails of a fox. And on the star's surface, I could see what resembled two menacing eyes glaring right at us, as it let out another yipping growl.

I narrowed my eyes at the sight, and I felt a chill shiver through me, as I recognized the feeling that the star's energy was eliciting. "Could this be the Fox Spirit calling out to us?"

"Perhaps," said the Spider.

As I pondered over this terrifying scenario before me, I couldn't help but think of my past encounters with the Fox Spirit down on my own world. How she was so bitter, how she had let her hatred and anger completely warp her view of the world. And now it appeared that even in defeat, she still wasn't through, as the negative energy that she had succumbed to had become so massive that it had seemingly manifested into the form of this star which now threatened our universe, much like the Fox Spirit once threatened our world.

"How could this be, though? And, what are we supposed to do to stop this?"

But then, those words popped into my head again, *"If you can't even find peace within yourself, then how can you hope to bring peace the world over?"*

I paused then, and my thoughts drifted to my own life. My actions in my life may have helped to bring about peace, but was I ever truly able to find peace within myself? They say that if you want peace, to prepare for war, and I realized that I really had been spending my whole life fighting. I couldn't help but wonder, is this what I had to look forward to? My own negative energy brewing into an unthinkable force of nature, destroying everything in its path?

Almost as if in response, I could feel another dreamlike memory come over me. And as I closed my eyes, I could see the memories of another past life flash before me.

4

Once upon a time, I was just a little kitten. I was one of several born in a litter of cats, and the people we were staying with were looking for homes for all of us. One day, a family came in to see us. It was three boys with their mom. And as they looked down at us, one of those boys happened to catch my eye, just as I appeared to catch his.

While the other two had picked out one of my brothers, this boy leaned down and scooped me into his arms. I latched my claws onto his shirt, and they peeled off like Velcro as he lifted me into the air. The boy named me then and there, and he told his mother that he wanted me all to himself.

That was the day that I met my boy.

A little while later, me and my brother, who they named Charlie, were brought home to our new family. My boy would pick me up and play with me all the time. He had a toy car that he would roll me around in sometimes, and when he'd carry me over his shoulder, he had a rat's tail on the back of his hair that I would like to bat at.

We were always trying to run outside whenever our people would open up the door, but they never let us out. That was too bad, because I could definitely use a break from my brother. Charlie was always a lot rougher at play. He'd scratch at our people, and he'd always take things a little too far with me, too. We really didn't get along too great, but at least I had my boy to always take care of me.

One day though, while being held in my boy's arms, I slipped from his grip, and I awkwardly fell to the ground. My body began shaking, and my boy was very concerned. He tried picking me back up, but I fell down again, and I couldn't stop shaking. Worried, he and his mother rushed me to the vet to make sure that I was okay. It turned out that I was fine, just especially shook. It was scary, but I was so glad to have my boy there with me the whole way through.

Back at home, my boy had built a small little room for just the two of us. He placed a blanket on the closet floor in the bedroom that he shared with his younger brother. I guess he needed an escape from his brothers, too. He made a small spot for me to stay near his clothes, and at night, the two of us would retreat to this small space. It was certainly cozy, but it was ours, where we could just escape from everyone and be at peace on our own.

* * *

Some time later, we moved to a new house. My boy managed to secure a bedroom all to himself, which gave the two of us a whole lot more space compared to the closet. And not only that, but at this new home, Charlie and I were finally allowed to go outside, too. That was especially nice, as with the new home, we gained a lot of new members to the family, as our people kept bringing home more and more new animals.

There were two dogs living there, and more cats than I care to count. My boy also brought home some new animals, including a rabbit, a couple of hamsters, and even a turtle at one point, but they were much smaller and more quiet, so they didn't bother me as much. As to the rest, though? Yeah, it was nice to be able to get out of the house and get away from everyone.

One day, I decided to sneak into the woods behind our house. There, I had caught sight of a small green lizard, which I began to stalk. I slowly approached, and as I moved, the leaves shifted.

The lizard stopped in its tracks, looking around for any threats. Noticing nothing out of the ordinary, it continued to scurry on.

I crept forward then, my eyes never leaving their target. When it appeared that the lizard had let its guard down, I scrunched down, ready to pounce.

"Rrrrrrrowr!"

I turned to the sound of the growl, but it was too late. A black tabby pounced out through the grass, tackling me and pinning me to the ground. Upon recognizing Charlie, I shoved him off and hissed at him.

He tried to chase me, but I managed to get away. I ran back home, just as my boy stepped outside to come looking for me. He scooped me up into his arms, and he brought me inside, taking us to our room.

My boy made a spot for me in a little bookshelf at the head of his bed. I'd lie down there and watch my boy go to sleep, and I'd usually groom his hair for him as he slept. It was nice having a peaceful place to get away from everyone each night.

* * *

We lived like this for many years, and I watched as my boy got older and eventually grew into a young man. One day though, he left home. He picked me up and hugged me, and he told me goodbye, but I really didn't understand what was happening at the time.

Days went by. Then weeks. Then months. But my boy didn't come back home.

I was sad. And I was lonely. Yes, me, the cat who likes to be left alone. During this period, I started spending more time in his mom's room, and she was able to comfort me and keep me company as best as she could. And though she tried, it just wasn't quite the same as with my boy.

I didn't know what happened to him. I wasn't sure if I was ever going to see him again. And it was the not knowing that tore at my heart the most.

But then one night, I was wandering around outside, walking along the backyard fence of our house. A car pulled up, and it stopped. I didn't pay it any mind though, even as someone stepped out of the car. Not until I heard my name being called.

"Velcro!"

I glanced over. And then I did a double take,

and I couldn't believe my eyes.

"Meow!"

I pranced over, and I was scooped into the arms of my boy. He was really here, he finally came back. He was wearing some sort of military uniform, which he was quick to change out of after bringing me home inside. He took me to bed with him in our room that night, and I purred and purred, as I slept peacefully next to my boy for the first time in what felt like forever.

* * *

Some time after my boy came home from the military for good, we moved out of his mom's house and into our own trailer. That first night was pretty scary, it was my first time moving away from home, and the place was completely empty, save for a sleeping bag for my boy. But he got the place furnished soon enough, and before I knew it, it was home sweet home.

Once more, I wasn't allowed out of the house. But this time it wasn't a big deal, because I had the whole place to myself. At least, until my boy eventually got another rabbit, but like before, he was quiet and he left me alone. But everything I could ever want was already in here, so what reason did I have to go outside?

It was pure bliss living here, just me and my boy. No other cats pestering me, no siblings bullying me. This was the life, and I was literally flipping from happiness. My boy liked to rough-house with me sometimes, such as when he'd wrestle with me, or wrap me around his shoulders or place me on his head, and I would always sigh and humor him for a moment before scrambling away. He'd also sometimes sneak up on me while I was laying down and rub my belly really rough. I'd quickly latch onto his arm and kick and bite at him when he'd do this, but then I'd stop and look him in the eye, and I'd start licking him to let him know that I was only playing, too.

Not one to always be on the recieving end, I had my own ways of getting back at my boy. He had a collection of comic books that I would constantly knock onto the floor, much to his chagrin. And I'd also sometimes bat around with other trinkets of his and make a bunch of noise while he was trying to sleep. It was all in good fun, though.

We were always there for each other. There were times when I might be taking a nap in the living room, but I could hear my boy was upset in the other room. So I'd get up and prance over to him to cheer him up, and I think I did a good job at that. Other times he'd get out of bed and gather me from the living room for comfort of his own accord, which I was okay with as well. And during the winter, some nights it would get really cold, but I always knew I could sneak under my boy's covers and cuddle up by his belly for warmth.

We really were inseperable. I felt like a kitten, even in my older age by this point. These were the happiest years of my life.

* * *

Eventually, we had to move back into his mom's house. I was saddened by this, but I made the best of it. The dogs were all gone, as were a number of the cats that used to live there, including my brother Charlie. Some new cats had moved in in the meantime, but I didn't bother trying to get to know them, and thankfully none of them bothered with me, either.

It wasn't long after moving back in that my health started to deteriorate though, and I grew really weak. My boy was very worried about me, and he took me to the vet to see if there was anything they could do to improve my condition. I was just very tired, and it was a struggle to move. I didn't even want to eat anymore. I just wanted to lay down and rest.

Some days later, my boy scooped me up into his arms, and he wrapped a towel around me. He took me into the car, where his father drove him to the doctor's office while he held me the entire way. We went inside, and the doctor brought out a needle. My boy stood up, and with tears in his eyes, he kissed me on the head and told me goodbye. The doctor stuck the needle in me, and soon, I was drifting to sleep, leaving this life with my boy the same way I had started it, being held in his arms. It was scary, but I was so glad to have my boy there with me the whole way through, and I couldn't help but feel an overwhelming sense of peace.

5

As I opened my eyes, I felt that overwhelming peace come over me, a satisfaction I didn't even know was possible before now. And yet I was finally able to experience it for myself, even if in another life.

In the time that I had been away experiencing the memory of that past life, the Fox Spirit's star had grown exponentially, increasing to such a gargantuan size that its diameter managed to close the distance that had been between us, to where now it was directly in front of me, red and angry and growling.

"Glad to have you back," said the Spider. "Did you come up with something while you were dreaming?"

Smiling, I nodded in response, and I reached out towards the star. I summoned all of that tranquility that resonated within me, and I let that energy spill out from my being, sharing it with the star.

"You don't have to keep holding onto all that hate," I whispered. "It's okay to let it go, and finally be at peace."

As I watched I could see the anger slowly slip away from the Fox Spirit's eyes. Its solar flare tails gradually simmered as their flailing subsided, and the Fox Spirit's growling quieted. When the entirety of the star's negative energy had been washed away, I gave one final push of my peaceful spirit, and we watched as the Fox Spirit's star began to glow a blinding light.

"Magnificent," spoke the Spider in awe.

Then the star exploded in an effervescent burst of serenity.

The power of the explosion was such that it sent me and the Spider flying backward through space.

Back through the galaxies.

Back past the other worlds.

Until we found ourselves back in our own solar system. The Spider landed back on our moon, but I continued in my descent, falling faster and faster, back down into the atmosphere of my world. And as I fell back first into the clouds like a comforting embrace, I could feel myself slipping away, drifting off to sleep with a smile on my face, and a newfound sense of peace born within me.

HOOK & LOOP
IN THE
REALM OF BEASTS

1

Loop was an orange haired girl, and Hook was her orange furred cat. These two gingers were sitting on a bench in the park in front of a small lake, and watching the busy bees bouncing from flower to flower as they waited. She liked watching the bees, it brought her a sense of peace, which was precisely what she needed in this moment, as her anxiety started to set in.

"He's late," Loop muttered, dropping her head in disappointment.

Hook hopped off the bench then, and he batted at the bees.

"Hey, stop that," Loop said. She leaned over and rolled Hook onto his back, and she started frantically rubbing his belly. "How do *you* like it, huh?"

Hook responded by latching his arms around hers, and he bit down on her while kicking his feet. After a moment he stopped, and he looked her in the eyes. Then he released his fangs and started licking her arm instead, showing that he was just being playful, too.

Loop stood up to her feet, sighing. "Well, I guess we better get going."

Hook meowed in response, and she lifted the cat up, holding him in her arms like a baby. Hook humored her for a moment, but then quickly scrambled out of her grasp and back down to his feet. As Loop stepped off, he followed after, rubbing against her legs and tripping her up.

"Goofball," she said, rolling her eyes. "At least I can always count on you."

The two were inseparable like this. They always had been ever since Hook was a little kitten, and their bond had only grown stronger over the years. They knew each other so well. They knew just how to get on each others nerves, and they knew how to cheer one another up, too. And Loop sure could use some cheering up, after her date had seemingly stood her up.

Then in an instant, a sudden burst of fire exploded from out of nowhere, and all of the plant life in the park lit up in flames.

Loop screamed, and she scooped Hook up into her arms and sprinted out of the park and back into town. There she saw that the fire had spread, as the streets were in flames and every building in sight was burning.

"This is horrible," Loop said, her eyes darting around at all of the carnage. But the more she looked around, the more she noticed that all of the people were still carrying on about their business like nothing had happened. Cars were still driving down the lit up roads, and people were still casually strolling down the sidewalk, seemingly oblivious to the chaos that surrounded them. "Huh?"

She then heard a loud screeching, and she looked up to see the skies were occupied with massive vultures flying around in circles, scouring for prey.

"You're seeing this, too, right?" she asked Hook, who was staring up with terrified eyes and his fur standing on end.

"Hurry, this way," she then heard someone yell, and she turned to see a group of smaller animals at the end of the block being lead back into the park by a brown tabby cat walking on his hind legs. "Quickly now, quickly," spoke the cat.

"Did... did that cat just speak?" Loop asked aloud.

The cat's ears twitched at the sound of her

voice, and he turned to see her staring at him. "Can you see me?" asked the cat.

"Yes, of course," said Loop. "What's going on?"

"There's no time," the cat said, exasperated. "Come on, we have to get out of here, before *they* spot us," he said, motioning to the vultures above.

Loop looked back up at the vultures. Then she looked back down to the cat, who was still waving her over. She shook her head in disbelief, then she ran to join the cat and the other animals back into the park. They rushed past the flames, and the cat lead them to a small cave opening that she had never noticed before. They quickly filed inside.

When it appeared the coast was clear, Loop took a breather and noticed all of the other smaller critters around them, all being guarded by a gaggle of geese.

"Is everyone alright?" the cat asked.

"What is this place?" asked Loop. "And what's going on out there? Why did nobody else seem to notice the fire or the vultures? And how are you able to talk?"

"Whoa whoa, one thing at a time," said the cat.

Hook hopped out of her arms, and he

approached the cat, sniffing him curiously.

"I'll explain everything shortly. But first, I think some introductions are in order." The cat extended a hand up to Loop. "My name is Rex, and I'm a guardian of the Realm of Spirits."

"Um..."

"... and you are?" asked Rex.

"I, uh, I'm Loop," she said, shaking Rex's hand. "And this here is Hook. And... just what in the heck is going on??"

2

"As I said," began Rex, "I'm a guardian of the Realm of Spirits. But recently, the Realm has come under attack. Upon arriving in the Realm, an evil spirit known as the Devil Dog used dark alchemy learned in his past life in order to forge a weapon, his trident, with which he is able to nullify the other spirits, and even take them under his control in certain instances. With this weapon, he has transformed the Realm of Spirits into the Realm of Beasts, a place where all who preside become his mindless minions. And ever since he's taken over the Realm of Spirits, he has planned to expand his territory."

"So that explains the fire, and what you all were running from," said Loop, "but that still doesn't explain why nobody else but me was able to see it."

"It's because *my* Realm has not yet merged

with *yours*. And until such a merging takes place, the people of your Realm will remain unaware, until it's too late. I've managed to save these young spirits for now," he said, referring to the other animals, "and we've been able to escape this far out. But the Devil Dog's vultures continue to follow us, and so the Devil Dog's pursuit continues."

"So then, what Realm is mine? And, why can *I* see you all?" asked Loop.

"Yours is the Realm of the Living," said Rex.

"The Living?" asked Loop. "So does that mean that you all *aren't* living?"

"Not exactly. Despite the name, it might be easier to think of it as a Realm of Humans. We *are* alive, but on a different plane of existence. However, it *is* a plane that you shouldn't be able to interact with," said Rex, who was eyeballing Hook. "Though I do have my theories as to how it is you've somehow managed to slip into our Realm."

Rex stared solemnly at Hook, leaving Loop to ponder about what Rex might be thinking.

"But anyways," Rex changed the subject, "we must find a way to stop the Devil Dog from expanding his territory any further, lest he succeed in merging the Realm of Beasts with the Realm of the Living and enslave all of humanity as well."

"Well how are we supposed to do that?"

asked Loop.

"With your help, there might just be a way."

"Wait, *my* help? What do you expect *me* to be able to do?"

"The powers of the Devil Dog's trident currently only affects other spirits," said Rex. "I myself am not a spirit, but a guardian of spirits, which is in part why I've been able to remain free to save whoever I've been able to. But *you* are also not a spirit, so perhaps you can help to aid in the fight to save our Realm.

"While the Devil Dog has taken many spirits under his control, there are others who are too powerful for him to control, who he has instead imprisoned. One such spirit that I have in mind is Ella, a blizzardous spirit who, should we succeed in freeing and returning her spiritual powers, could have the potential to undo all of the Devil Dog's progress so far."

"Okay," said Loop. "So, how do we go about freeing this Ella?"

"We need to travel to the Realm of Beasts," said Rex. "From there, we'll seek out the caverns where Ella and the others are being held prisoner. We then find Ella, break her out, and confront the Devil Dog and destroy his trident, all while trying to avoid any beasts along the way."

"Wow," said Loop. "You make all of that sound so easy."

"Did you not hear the part about avoiding the beasts and confronting the Devil Dog??"

"How do you know all of this stuff anyways?" Loop asked.

"Because I've been sneaking about doing what I can to save who I can, but I can only do so much."

"So, the Devil Dog's weapon won't affect me, but still, how do you expect me to take on these powerful beasts? After all, *you're* not able to, apparently."

"Well hopefully we won't have to," said Rex. "However, should it come to that, I have a feeling that you'll be more up to the task than you think."

"Okay, you need to stop with the cryptic talk and just come out with it," said Loop. "What are you holding back from me?"

Rex sighed. "*Fine*, though it is just a theory. But I have a feeling that your cat Hook is in fact a spirit animal."

"*What?*" Loop gasped.

"Yes, but not just any spirit animal, *your* spirit animal. Which would mean that you should possess his spiritual powers, even though you are not a spirit yourself."

"Huh. And why do you think this exactly?"

"Why else would you two be able to interact with me right now?" asked Rex. "Why, if not because you were already tapped into your inner beast?"

3

Loop and Hook were riding atop the back of one of the geese, with Rex flying along on the back of a second goose beside them. The pair flew them out of the park and out of town. And as they approached their destination, both Hook and Loop's eyes widened in amazement as they saw where the geese were taking them.

"*Wow!*"

It was an island floating in the sky, and it was massive.

Her wonder soon turned to horror the closer they got, as she could see that the island was a deserted fiery wasteland.

The geese landed on the island's edge. As the trio hopped off, the geese were quick to say their farewells and fly away again.

"Where are they going?" asked Loop. "Aren't they coming with us?"

"It isn't safe for them, not with the vultures about. It's best that they head back to the cave and keep watch over the younger spirits," said Rex. "Also, I must mention, there is another spirit who's been taken under the Devil Dog's control that we must watch out for. His name is Eagle Eye, and he's a bald eagle who keeps watch from the sky for roamers such as us. We can only hope that we haven't been spotted already."

Rex then handed Loop a small satchel. She opened it up and pulled out a desert camouflaged cloak.

"Put this on," said Rex, taking a second cloak out for himself. "It'll help keep us hidden, and also acts as a fire blanket to protect us from the flames."

With Hook still sitting on her shoulder, Loop threw the cloak over the both of them, then she and Rex huddled close to the ground as they made their move with Rex leading the way. Cautiously they maneuvered across the dangerous terrain, until they finally arrived at their target location, just on the edge of a valley.

"We're here," said Rex, standing up and taking off his cloak.

"Okay, but where's here?" asked Loop, as she put away her own cloak.

"This is the great lake of the Realm of Spirits," said Rex.

"But... there's no lake here," said Loop.

"That's because it's been drained of all its water since becoming the Realm of Beasts. But we still must make our way to the bottom, for that's the way inside the island's inner workings."

Hook hopped off of Loop's shoulder, and the three of them began their climb down into the valley. They didn't make it far though before they heard a screech from up above. They all turned up just in time to see a massive bald eagle swooping down towards them. Before they could even react, it quickly snatched Hook within its talons and swooped back up in the air.

"No! Hook!" screamed Loop.

She and Rex scrambled back out of the valley, but all they could do was stare up in terror as the eagle flew higher above them.

"This is no good," said Rex. "That's Eagle Eye."

"What do we do?" asked Loop, desperately.

"We have faith," Rex reassured.

They watched as Hook wriggled around in the eagle's grasp. He bared his claws, then went to work scratching his way out. Finally Eagle Eye released him, and Hook let out a yowl as he plummeted back to the ground.

"Hook!"

Loop reached up for her cat and she managed to catch him, falling down on her back from the impact. "Oh Hook," she said, hugging her shaken cat close, as tears began to well in her eyes.

"Come on, we have to go," said Rex.

Loop rolled back to her feet, her cat still in her arms, and she asked, "Now what?"

Rex turned back to the sky, where Eagle Eye was already circling back around towards them. "Now, we *run*."

With Hook still in her arms, Loop and Rex dodged and weaved as they hurried toward the valley's bottom. Eagle Eye let out a wailing screech, and Loop turned to look in terror.

"Don't stop," warned Rex, and Loop heeded the cat's words.

Once at the bottom, they approached what little water remained in a small puddle.

"Quickly now, jump in."

"Wha..." but before Loop could finish her thought, Rex had already hopped into the puddle, disappearing with a splash. "O-okay," Loop said. She exchanged a glance with Hook, then they heard the piercing screech up above again. The two stared up with widened gazes, and their jaws dropped at the sight of Eagle Eye swooping back down to them.

Loop let out a scream, then she closed her eyes and took a leap of faith into the puddle of water. Once on the other side, she landed hard on her butt on the rocky ground, which cut her screams short. "Ouch! What the...?"

She opened her eyes and looked up to see that the water they had jumped into was somehow still on the ceiling.

"We should be safer down here, from Eagle Eye at least," said Rex. "Though there'll be more obstacles awaiting us yet, so stay on your guard."

He helped Loop up to her feet. Hook hopped out of her arms, and the two of them followed Rex as they headed down a dark rocky tunnel. As they moved forward, she could hear a faint sound coming from up ahead, like a series of shrieking chirps.

"What's that?" asked Loop.

"Get down," said Rex, and the shrieks quickly grew louder and more abundant. "Bats!"

They soon found themselves overrun by a flapping swarm of bats. Loop screamed as she ducked down, and Hook swatted his paws to ward them off. Soon the bats had passed, and their shrieks could be heard receding in the distance.

"Alright, let's keep moving," said Rex, and they got back to their feet and continued forward.

Loop noticed as the temperature had increased, and sweat began dripping down her face. Soon they found themselves standing just outside a room in the cave in which the floor was covered in lava. "Oh," said Loop. "So, uh, what's the plan now?"

Rex hopped to a rock slab jutting up from the lava, then motioned for Loop and Hook to follow.

"You're kidding me, right?" asked Loop.

"Not at all," said Rex, hopping to another rock slab. "Now come on, no time to lose."

Loop was unconvinced, until Hook sprang into action, leaping out to the first rock slab. "Hook!" Loop screamed, nearly having a heart attack until he landed safely on the rock. "Not you, too," she sighed. "Well, here goes nothing."

She braced herself, then she leaped out, landing beside her cat. They stood up, then hopped to the next rock, following the path that Rex had traversed. Once they successfully crossed the lava and made it to the other side of the room, Loop knelt over panting after the blazing excursion.

"Come, let's step away from the lava," said Rex, urging Loop and Hook to join him into the next passageway of the cave system. He retrieved a pair of torches, and handed one over to Loop.

"So how many more of these obstacles are we going to have to cross?" Loop asked.

"It should be a relatively straight shot from here," said Rex. "Just a little ways further and we should be where they're keeping the spirits prisoner."

The cave began to rumble then, and the trio stopped in their tracks.

"Um, Rex?"

"Oh this isn't good," said Rex. "Quick, we have to get out of here!"

The three sprinted forward at Rex's command, when rocks started falling from the cave's ceiling.

"It's going to cave in," said Loop.

"Which is why we must *hurry*."

Loop looked up and saw a larger rock fall. It narrowly missed her, but it fell just in the way of Hook's path, stalling the cat.

"Hook!" she screamed, but as she stopped, even more rocks fell before she could reach her cat.

Rex was able to hop to Hook's side just in time before a wall of rocks fell, which cut the two cats off from Loop.

"Hook!" she yelled again. "Rex! Can you

hear me?"

"Yes, I can still hear you," Rex responded. "Don't worry, we're both okay. We managed to miss being hit by the rocks."

"Oh thank goodness," said Loop. "Well how are you two going to get over here?"

"Loop, just wait for us there, we'll have to circle around and find another way."

"What, you want me to just sit here and wait? But what if the cave starts moving again? Rex?"

But there was no response, as Rex and Hook had apparently already set off to find another path.

"Well that's just great," Loop moped.

She then heard another rumbling. Worried about another cave in, she started sprinting down the corridor. But as she ran, she noticed that the room didn't appear to be shaking like before, and she slowed down, hearing the rumbling sound echoing off the cave walls. She cautiously moved forward, unable to see clearly in the dark as she waved her torch in front of her. Then as she made it to the end of the corridor, she found herself at a dead end.

"Uh-oh," said Loop. "I hope I'm not trapped down here."

She pressed her hand against the wall, trying

to push her way through. But then the rumbling sound stopped, and a giant eye opened where the wall was, staring directly at Loop.

4

Loop stared back at the eye, then she heard a growling. The beast then stepped away from the cave opening, revealing itself to be a gigantic lizard, who continued to stare down at her grumpily. Loop realized then that the rumbling sounds she was hearing must have been this creature snoring, and she had to go and wake him up.

Loop took a step back, and then another, and then she turned to run back into the cave hall. The lizard reached in and snatched her by the leg, though, and Loop dropped her torch as she fell to the ground. The lizard then dragged Loop out of the hall and into the wide open area of the cave. She kicked the lizard off, and she scrambled back to her feet. Then she noticed there were metal bars that were covering up various holes in the wall behind the lizard.

"This must be where they're keeping the spirits prisoner," Loop surmised.

She then engaged in a stand off with the giant lizard, and she gulped at the sight before her.

"What did Rex say before, something about Hook being my spirit animal?" she whispered to herself. "Well if that's true, then maybe I should just do what Hook would do."

She took a deep breath. Then she let out a battle cry and charged for the lizard. She reared back her arm, then she swiped forward, scratching at the beast like a cat.

It didn't appear to have any effect. And when Loop looked up, the lizard had an annoyed look on his face.

"Well that didn't work."

The lizard then grabbed Loop by the arm, and it raised her into the air just in front of his mouth. Loop looked on terrified as the lizard opened his jaws and screamed ferociously in her face.

* * *

Loop sat locked away in one of the rocky prison cells, anxious about her current predica-ment. "I hope Hook and Rex are doing better than I am," she thought aloud, and let out a worried sigh.

"You're not from here, are you?" she heard someone say from the neighboring cell.

"No, I'm not," said Loop, wrapping her arms around her legs. "I'm not a spirit animal, or an inner beast, or anything special like that. I'm just a regular girl. A girl who got stood up by her date, and then separated from her best friend, with no foreseeable way to get back to him."

"I wouldn't beat yourself up so badly," said the neighbor. "You're stronger than you realize to even make it this far. Even *my* powers were no match for what we're up against, and I'm locked away just like you. Tell me, what's your name, girl?"

"I'm Loop," she said. Then, suddenly curious about her neighbor, she asked, "Wait, who are you?"

Her neighbor responded, "I'm Ella."

"Oh wow, you're exactly who we came here looking for," Loop said excitedly.

"A wasted effort, I'm sad to say," said Ella.

"What do you mean?"

"It's no use. I'm powerless to do anything against the Devil Dog, not so long as he still possesses that weapon of his."

"Well that's the thing," said Loop. "We

didn't just come here to break you out. We also intended to destroy that weapon, so that you can use your powers to restore the Realm of Spirits."

"You make that sound so easy," said Ella.

"That's exactly what I told Rex," said Loop.

"Oh, Rex is still out there?"

"Well yes," said Loop. "How else would I have made it this far?"

"I was worried that he'd been captured," said Ella. "After all, they already succeeded in capturing his spirit animal."

"You mean Rex's spirit animal is locked away here with us, too?"

"Not exactly," said Ella. "He's the one keeping us locked in here."

"You mean..."

"Yes, that lizard you encountered, that's Rex's spirit animal, taken under the control of the Devil Dog."

"Oh no," Loop shuddered. "Well how do we get past him?"

"If anyone knows, it'll be Rex," said Ella.

Just then, they heard the click of a lever being pulled, and the metal bars holding them in began to slide open.

"You're not wrong about that," Loop heard Rex say, as he and Hook stepped into view.

"You made it!" Loop said, rushing over to Hook and scooping him into her arms. "I was so worried," she said, hugging her cat close.

"We found another way thankfully. But more to the point, my spirit animal, Trevor, is quite a mighty foe. But like me, he also tries to fit in as many naps as he can, so we'd best get going before he wakes up again."

"Wait, that big monster's name is Trevor?"

"Yes, or Tee for short."

Loop then looked over as Ella stepped out of her cell. She was surprised to see that Ella was a giant, majestic duck.

"It's wonderful to see you again, Rex," said Ella.

"And you, Ella," said Rex.

"Alright, so where to next?" asked Loop.

"Next, we're going to the island's core to confront the Devil Dog."

Rex lead the way out of the prison area, but they were met by the lizard Tee who was waiting for them. He wore an even grumpier expression than before after having been reawakened once more.

"Darn," said Rex. "Also like me, he's quite a light sleeper."

"So now what?" asked Loop.

"We outrun the beast!"

They attempted to high tail it out of there, but Tee was quick to block their path with his tail.

"It's no use," said Rex. "We're not going to be able to get around him. We're going to have to take him down in order to pass."

"But how?" asked Loop.

Hook then let out a battle meow, and he charged toward the lizard. He reared back his paw, then swiped out with his claws, but his attack had no effect on Tee.

"I tried that already," said Loop.

"His body is virtually bulletproof," said Rex. "We're going to have to try a different tactic to bring him down."

Loop thought about it for a moment, then she and Hook looked at each other, as an idea had arrived in both their minds at the same time. She called a huddle, and whispered her plan to Hook, Rex, and Ella.

"That just might work," said Rex.

"Great. So everyone got it?" asked Loop.

"Let's do it," said Ella.

They sprang into action, as Loop hopped onto Ella's back, and Ella rose into the air, flying up to Tee's face. They floated around like a fly, irritating the lizard, as he stood on his hind legs and swatted out at them. However, Ella was able to evade his strikes with grace.

On the ground, Hook and Rex then rubbed up against the beast's legs, tripping him up. The lizard tried to catch his balance, when Ella flew straight for his head, knocking Tee down hard onto his back. The room shook from the impact of his fall.

Ella then hovered in the air high above Tee's stomach, and Loop hopped off. She landed on his stomach like a cannonball, which made the lizard groan in pain.

"It worked," said Loop, hopping back onto the ground as Ella landed beside her.

"Yes, but we might be in for a different sort of trouble," Rex said, as the room continued to rumble.

"Oh man, we're not about to get caved in again, are we?" asked Loop.

A hole then blasted up from the floor, startling the whole group.

"What's all this commotion up here about?" they heard a voice speak, followed by a small dachshund dog climbing out of the hole.

"That's not the Devil Dog, is it?" asked Loop.

"Of course not," said Rex, "just one of his

many minions."

They then heard another voice booming up from the hole, telling the dachshund, "Out of the way."

The dachshund did as commanded, and out climbed a menacing figure. He was a ripped pit bull with fire in his eyes and horns on his head, and he wielded a black trident in his hand.

"*That's* the Devil Dog," said Rex.

5

The Devil Dog looked over to Tee laid out on his back. "Impressive," he said, nodding his head. "I wouldn't expect you lot would be able to take him out. But I promise you, I won't go down so easily."

He readied his trident, and Loop and the others took a fighting stance. Ella then reared back her wings, and she thrust forward a gust of icy wind. The Devil Dog blocked the blow with his trident though, then shot out a fiery beam that knocked Ella off her feet.

"Ella!" screamed Loop.

"That's his weapon that we have to destroy," said Rex, rushing over to Ella's side. "We're hopeless to defeat him so long as he continues to wield it."

"Right," said Loop. She then nodded down to Hook. "Alright, are you ready? Let's do this."

She balled up her fists, and right after Hook hopped up onto her shoulder, she charged at the menacing Devil Dog. Hook then leaped out, swiping his claws at the Devil Dog's face. The Devil Dog evaded the strike, but Loop quickly followed up with a hard punch that caught him right on the jaw.

For a moment, the Devil Dog looked stunned. But then he laughed off her efforts. "I really hope that you can do better than that."

He then tapped the bottom of his trident against the floor, and a burst of fire blasted up from the ground just in front of Loop, sending her and Hook reeling backwards. The Devil Dog then reached through the fire and grabbed Loop by her orange hair, and he pulled her up off the ground and laughed mockingly in her face.

Hook leaped up and latched hold of the Devil Dog's arm, and he bit down and went to work rapidly kicking, trying to tear the dog's arm to shreds. The Devil Dog merely flung the cat away though, then turned his attention back to Loop with a smirk.

"It's going to take a lot more than some mere scratches from your pet cat to do me any harm."

Hook wasn't done yet though, and he sprinted back over to the Devil Dog, this time sinking his claws into his legs and biting down on his ankle.

"Grr," the Devil Dog grumbled. Thoroughly annoyed, the Devil Dog let go of Loop, then he kicked Hook into the air. He grabbed the cat by the throat, then chokeslammed him down to the hard rocky ground. He then pulled the cat back up and tossed him away effortlessly.

Hook landed lifeless to the ground, and Loop watched on with horror in her eyes. "Hook!"

She scrambled over to her cat's side. She got down to her knees, and tried urging Hook to wake up. He was unresponsive. "No, Hook," she said, as tears formed in her eyes.

Rex and Ella got back to their feet, and they lowered their heads in respect for the apparently lifeless cat.

"Pathetic," the Devil Dog scoffed.

Loop was struck by the Devil Dog's ugly remark. She stood back up to her feet, and her grief transitioned to anger and hatred. She clenched her fists, and she tightened her jaw. Her body began to shake, and tiger stripes began forming all over. She then snapped her head in the Devil Dog's direction, showing off her ferocious eyes which had become like that of a cat's.

"Now *this* is interesting," the Devil Dog said

with malicious amusement.

Loop growled under her breath, and then she charged for the Devil Dog. She reared back her arm, and she revealed the razor sharp claws that had sprung from her fingertips.

She roared, swiping out at the Devil Dog, but he dodged backwards to avoid the attack. No matter, Loop pounced forward, knocking her foe off his feet.

He looked up in fear as she raised her claws into the air. He raised his trident to block her strike, but as she struck down, the blow was so powerful she snapped the trident in two.

"No!" the Devil Dog shouted. He shoved Loop off of him and returned to his feet, staring down in disbelief at the pieces of his broken trident. He was steaming mad, and as he tossed his trident aside, he glared down at Loop and prepared to end her with one final attack.

"Enough playing around, it's time to finish this."

Ella had recovered though, and she once again reared back her wings. She thrust them at him, blasting him with a blizzardous gust of frigid wind. Her power was such that it froze the Devil Dog in place like an ice statue.

Loop then picked up the sharp end of the

trident piece, and she rushed forward. She let out another roar and stabbed the Devil Dog with it, and his body shattered from the impact. Loop then stared down at the remains of the Devil Dog, her shoulders rising and falling with every heavy breath.

She then dropped down to her knees, and she fell to her hands. And as she broke down sobbing, her stripes faded away, her claws rescinded back into her fingers, and her eyes returned to normal.

"Me... ow..." she heard weakly behind her.

Loop snapped up at the sound of the meow, then she turned around to look at her cat. "Hook?"

And she saw as Hook had awakened, and was fighting to get back to his feet.

"Hook!"

She ran over to her cat and hugged him in tight. He meowed in pain though, so she loosened her grip, as her tears of sorrow turned to tears of happiness. "Goofball. I can always count on you."

6

Rex reunited with Tee, now that the Devil Dog's spell was broken, and the two of them freed all the other beasts who were still being held prisoner. Ella used her powers to put out the Devil Dog's fires on the island's surface, then the other magical beasts helped out in refilling the great lake, and then replenishing the green forest that had been torched to the ground.

They all then heard a loud screeching sound from above, and down swooped Eagle Eye. Loop and Hook initially went on their guard, but the bald eagle landed in front of them and knelt forward, allowing Loop to pat his crest.

With the Realm of Spirits fully restored, Loop and Hook then said their farewells to their new friends.

"Will we ever see you again?" Loop asked Rex.

"I suppose it's possible, even if in another lifetime," Rex said.

Ella and Tee then joined Rex in saying goodbye to Loop and Hook. One of the geese helped transport them back to the park, where they found that the Devil Dog's fires had also already been put out. After saying his goodbyes, the goose then helped guide some of the younger spirits back up to the Realm of Spirits, leaving Loop and Hook back at the bench where they had started.

Loop then looked down, and she watched as the busy bees continued to bounce from flower to flower. Rather than peace, though, this time the sight brought back a bleak reminder.

"Oh yeah, we've still been stood up," Loop remembered.

Hook rubbed against her legs, trying to console her, when they heard another cat meowing in the distance. The two of them looked up, and they saw as a guy and his cat were quickly approaching them.

"Hey, sorry I'm late," said the young fellow. "I got caught up with something, but I hope I haven't kept you waiting too long."

"Oh, it's no biggie," said Loop, with a smile on her face. Then, with a wink to her cat, "We actually got caught up with a little something, too."

CHLOE AND THE GUACAMOLE

Mom came home one night with a bag of food in hand. As she sat down to eat, the fluffy gray cat Chloe hopped up onto the table to see what Mom had brought home. She saw that Mom was eating a sandwich, and she was eating chips with her meal. Chloe leaned in to sniff the chips, and Mom gave her one to munch on, which she happily obliged. Chloe fell in love with the taste, and she purred in delight at the tasty treat.

Over the next few days, as Mom would sit down to eat, she'd have a bag of chips open to munch on with her meal. And every time, Chloe would hop on the table and meow until Mom gave in and shared the chips with her.

Then one day, instead of her usual sandwich, Mom brought home quesadillas. And this time, to go with her chips, Mom had brought home some sort of green dip. She called it guacamole, and she'd dip her chips into it before each bite. Chloe tried sniffing at the guacamole, but

Mom was hesitant to let her try it. She shooed Chloe away, and let her munch on bare chips. And Chloe enjoyed her chips as usual, but Mom not letting her try them with the guacamole only piqued her curiosity.

Mom got up, and Chloe watched as she left the room. Her eyes then darted at the guacamole, and her intrigue got the better of her. She sniffed it first, then glanced to make sure that Mom was still out of the room. Then she leaned in, and she lapped up a chunk of the green substance into her mouth. As the guacamole hit her tongue, Chloe's eyes widened in amazement at the delicious taste.

Then suddenly, a puff of smoke erupted around Chloe. When the smoke cleared, Chloe was still sitting on the table. However, as she looked down, she saw that her gray furry legs and paws had been replaced by human arms and hands. And as she inspected herself all over, she realized that she was now wearing gray colored clothing, and she was no longer a cat, but had somehow transformed into a human woman with gray colored hair.

"Holy guacamole!" Chloe uttered.

Then Mom entered back into the room. She glanced up at Chloe, then jumped with a startle.

"Aah! Who are you? What are you doing in

my house?" Mom shouted, and chased the woman down. "Get out! Get out!"

Chloe ran in fear, rushing out of the house, and Mom slammed the door shut behind her. Chloe hid in the bushes when police arrived, and Mom stepped outside to talk to them, explaining what had just transpired, still shaken by the altercation. Chloe felt bad for making Mom so scared, but she wasn't entirely sure what was going on with her, either. Then a puff of smoke erupted around Chloe once more, and after it cleared, Chloe was back to being a cat again.

She let out a meow, and caught the attention of Mom. She scurried out of the bushes, and scampered to the front door, where Mom knelt down and scooped Chloe into her arms.

"She must have gotten outside when that woman ran out," Mom said, shaking her head.

The police officer informed Mom that they'd be on the lookout for her, and encouraged her not to worry too much before they went on their way. Mom brought Chloe back in the house, closing the door behind her, and hugging the cat comfortingly.

* * *

Later that night, after Mom had gone to bed,

Chloe sneaked back to the kitchen. Carefully, she pried open the refrigerator door, then she scoured the fridge for the guacamole. Upon locating the container on a middle shelf, she pawed at it, batting it until it fell from its shelf and onto the floor, popping the lid open in the process. Chloe looked around to ensure that the coast was still clear, then she lowered her head into the container, and she took a big bite of the delicious green treat.

With an eruption of smoke, Chloe once again transformed into her human state. Again checking to make sure nobody had heard her, she pressed the lid back on the container and placed it back on the shelf. Carefully she closed the door shut, then she sauntered over to a nearby window. Quietly, she opened the window, and then she let herself out to wander into the night.

She wandered down the streets with a sense of curiosity, admiring her human form with awe as she walked. Suddenly the sound of music captured her attention, and as she approached the music, she could make out a mariachi band performing a song inside of a Mexican restaurant.

Chloe stepped inside, where she was greeted by a waitress named Michelle.

"Hi, dining by yourself tonight?"

"Um, yes?" Chloe responded with uncertainty.

"Follow me," Michelle said with a smile, and she escorted Chloe to a small table. "Can I get you started with something to drink?"

Realizing she had grown parched from the walk, Chloe nodded her head in response. "Yes, please, some water would be great."

"Sure thing. And were you ready to order?"

"Order? Hmm..." Chloe pondered the question, when a familiar scent crept into her nostrils. "Ooh, what is that smell?" Her eyes then followed as another waitress walked past with a plate of quesadillas in hand. "Oh, I will have that please."

"Sure thing, one order of quesadillas coming right up." Michelle then stepped away before returning with the water, and she placed a basket of chips and a bowl of salsa onto the table as well. "Complimentary with your meal," she said with a wink, then wandered away.

Chloe inspected the chips, leaning in and sniffing them. She then grabbed a chip from the basket, and she took a bite. It was just like the ones Mom had fed her before. She then glanced over at the salsa, and she dipped her next chip in. She brought the chip with salsa up to her nose to smell it, then she took a bite. Her eyes widened in amazement, and she was floored by the wonderful taste.

She quickly ate the rest of her chips and salsa, looking like a maniac as she devoured them. By the time Michelle had returned with her meal, she had completely emptied the basket of chips.

"Oh my," said Michelle. "You finished all the chips and salsa? You must be pretty hungry."

She then placed the quesadillas in front of Chloe, and Chloe looked down curiously at the new plate of food in front of her.

"Enjoy!" said Michelle with a smile, leaving Chloe to her meal.

Much like the chips and salsa, Chloe first inspected the quesadillas with her nose. She then picked up a piece, and she took a bite. Chloe was in heaven. She instantly understood why Mom liked these so much, and she quickly scarfed the rest of the meal down with delight.

She leaned back in her chair afterwards, wrapping her arms around her full belly as she let out a satisfied sigh. Then a puff of smoke erupted, and Chloe was back to being a cat once more, as she awkwardly stumbled off of the chair and onto the floor.

When she noticed Michelle making her way back, Chloe quickly slunk over to the exit. Michelle looked confused by her sudden absence, as Chloe made her way back out onto the streets and started back for home after her scrumptious evening adventure.

* * *

The following night, after Mom had gone to bed, Chloe sneaked back to the kitchen again. However, this time she was startled to find the big orange cat Tom sitting beside the refrigerator, waiting patiently for her. Tom communicated with Chloe that he witnessed her sneaking out the previous night. However, she needn't worry, he wouldn't tell on her. All that he asked in return is that on this night, she let him join her. Chloe thought about it for a moment, then agreed to let the big cat tag along.

Tom helped Chloe pry the refrigerator door open, then she once again batted the container of guacamole onto the floor. After popping the lid off, first Chloe took a bite, then she transformed into a human in a puff of smoke. She then motioned for Tom to go next, and so he did. And in a puff of smoke, he too transformed into a human, only he was wearing orange clothing and had orange colored hair.

"Holy guacamole!" Tom exclaimed.

Chloe bonked him on the head, and pressed a finger to her lips, motioning for him to keep quiet.

"Oh, right," Tom whispered. "Sorry."

She then lead him to the same window she had sneaked out of the previous night, and the two of them slipped out and made their way down the street towards the sound of the mariachi music. Once they arrived at the Mexican restaurant, the two stepped inside, where they were greeted by their waitress, Michelle.

"Back again?" she asked Chloe, with a leery look in her eye. "And I see you've brought a friend tonight. Follow me right this way," she said, and she lead them to their table. "What can I get you two started to drink?"

"Water would be great," said Chloe, and Tom nodded in agreement. Michelle then stepped away before returning with the waters, and she placed a basket of chips and a bowl of salsa onto the table as well. "Are you two ready to order?"

"I'll have some guacamole," said Tom excitedly.

"Sure thing, and what'll you have with your guac?" asked Michelle.

"Uh..."

"We will both have quesadillas, please," answered Chloe.

"Sure thing, two orders of quesadillas, coming right up!"

As Tom scarfed down on the chips and salsa, Chloe leaned in and whispered to him. "We should be careful eating any more guacamole. We do not know how long its effects will last."

"Why does it matter?" asked Tom. "This is great being human! All the chips and salsa we can eat, and we don't even have to beg for it!"

But Chloe was uncertain.

After Michelle returned with their meals, Tom then switched up from dipping his chips in the salsa to dipping them in the guacamole. "Oh my lordy, this is delicious! You've gotta try it, Chloe!"

"Hmm," she pondered, then cautiously picked up a chip. "Well, okay," and she dipped her chip in the guacamole, and gave it a bite. "Oh my, you are right! This is truly heaven!"

The two then scarfed down the whole bowl of guacamole, before moving on to their quesadillas. After their meal, the two leaned back and patted their full bellies in satisfaction.

"*Ahem*," they then heard, and they turned to see a tall man who appeared to be the restaurant's owner standing at the table with his arms crossed. "I hope you two were planning to pay for your dinner tonight."

"Pay?" asked Chloe.

"What's that?" asked Tom.

"I figured as much, after you skipped out on your bill last night, young lady," said the man. "Sorry to say, but we don't run a free service here. If you two can't pay, then we're going to have to put you to work."

"*What?*" asked Chloe.

"*Work?*" uttered Tom.

"That's right," said the owner. "Now no more fussin', we've got some dishes that need cleaning."

After several hours of washing dishes, Chloe and Tom were finally allowed to leave, but not before being warned that they had better bring some money with them next time.

"Ah man, Chloe, that was awful," said Tom on their sad walk of shame back home. "Maybe being human isn't all it's cracked up to be after all."

"Yes, I much prefer being a cat," agreed Chloe. "Mom never makes us work for our food."

By the time they arrived home, the effects of the guacamole had finally worn off, and the two returned to their natural cat forms with a poof.

They sneaked back into the house, carefully closing the window behind them, then a very tired Chloe and Tom wandered to their separate resting spots to lay down and get some much needed sleep.

* * *

The days passed by, and life went back to normal for Chloe. Mom would come home from work and bring home some food, and Chloe would hop onto the table and ask her to share. Mom was usually one to oblige, until one night she once again came home with her favorite dish, the quesadillas with the chips and guacamole. Chloe was hesitant to join Mom, but the scent of the yummy meal roused her appetite, and she couldn't help herself.

Mom gave Chloe some of her chips, and Chloe eagerly ate them up. Mom then dipped one of her chips into the bowl of guacamole, but stopped just as she brought it to her mouth. She noticed Chloe staring at her, and then offered the chip with guac to the cat. Chloe leaned in to sniff it, and her curiosity started to swell.

THE OCEAN
AND THE MOON

The ever curious Josie, a fluffy black tabby, was outside staring up at the night sky with wonder.

"What's caught your eye?" asked the black and white Elder Stan, who approached the young kitten and joined her in looking up at the sky.

"I'm looking at the moon, Elder Stan," said Josie. "I was just thinking about how lonely it must be up there all by itself."

"Hmm, it's true that the moon can be lonely, but that's not always the case," said Elder Stan.

"What do you mean?" asked Josie.

"Once upon a time, the moon actually came down here to visit," he said.

"*Really?*" asked Josie in amazement, and Elder Stan began his story...

* * *

The Moon was very lonely up in space all by

himself. One thing that kept his loneliness at bay, though, was the sight of the Ocean on the planet below him. She caught the Moon's attention once he noticed his gravitational pull had an effect on her current. The Ocean was teeming with a whole world of life, from the myriad of fish in her depths, to the people sailing on the surface of her seas. And yet, despite all this life pulling her attention in different directions, still she always gravitated towards him, and it was like she was waving up at him, inviting him to join her.

Over the years, as his loneliness set in, the Moon continued to pine for that connection. He had only had a few visitors, and eventually even they had stopped coming. He fell in love with the sight of the Ocean though, and he very much had a desire to meet her up close.

And so one night, he decided to do just that.

On a night in which his usual shine was invisible in the sky, he slipped his consciousness and drifted down to the planet's surface. He took on the form of an illuminated handsome duck, and he approached the Ocean with intent.

"Dear Ocean," he spoke, "I am the Moon, finally come down to meet you. Won't you grant me your company on this clear starry night?"

At first, the Ocean appeared to ignore his wishes.

But then, from off in the distance, he noticed something approaching over the horizon. It was a gorgeous, graceful swan, the Ocean's choice of form with which to greet the Moon.

"Hello, dear Moon," said the Ocean. "I've noticed you watching me over the years, and I too must admit to having hoped to meet you one day. Come, swim with me, won't you?"

The duck stepped into the Ocean, swimming up beside the swan. The swan then flew in the air, and the duck followed, gliding up next to her just above the water, beaming as the Ocean's waves splashed up against his feathers.

They flew out into the middle of the sea, where the swan suddenly dove down into the water. The duck landed on the water, uncertain whether he should follow, when the swan suddenly popped back out and invited the duck down under. The duck dove in after her, and they were practically weightless beneath the Ocean's waves, not unlike being on the Moon's silvery surface.

After their midnight swim, the duck and the swan both floated on the Ocean's gentle swells. The swan looked up at the stars in the sky, but the duck couldn't keep his eyes off of his beloved. She noticed this, and looked back at him bashfully.

"Unfortunately I can't stay here, though I'd certainly love to," the Moon then spoke.

"I understand," said the Ocean. "Next time, I'll come up to visit you."

"I'd love that."

"But before you go back, just know that I love you, my Moon."

"And I love you, my Ocean," said the Moon.

The duck and the swan shared a kiss then, just as the Moon's consciousness began dissolving away back to his home in space high above.

The Ocean never did come up to visit the Moon, though he continued to keep watch over her all the same. He saw as she drifted away, which he supposed was understandable, given all the life pulling her attention in every which way. But he was sad all the same, and for a time the loneliness began to set back in.

Before, the Moon never really paid much attention to all the life on the Ocean, so blinded was he by his love for her. However, as he looked down now, he saw as people turned their eyes up to him. He saw them pointing up at him, smile at him, staring at him in awe. And for the first time in a very long time, suddenly, the Moon didn't feel so lonely anymore.

* * *

"So you see, the moon isn't as alone as it

seems," concluded Elder Stan. "It's got all of us to watch over, just like you have your family, and just like I have all of you, too."

"Wow, that's amazing, Elder Stan," exclaimed Josie. And as she turned her gaze back to the sky, she smiled under the moon's light with glee.

GOODBYE,
ELDER STAN

Minnie, Mickey, Josie, and Daisy were all gathered and keeping a watchful eye over Elder Stan. Stan had been feeling especially weak recently, and found he spent more time than usual resting in bed.

"How are you feeling today, Elder Stan?" asked the short haired brown kitten, Minnie.

"Are you doing any better?" asked the big fluffy brown kitten, Daisy.

"Oh, I am grateful to see you kittens," Elder Stan responded through tired eyes. "You all didn't happen to see my wife, Zoe, on your way in, did you?"

"We didn't," said the fluffy black kitten Josie with a frown, and Elder Stan looked sad.

"What's wrong, Elder Stan?" asked Minnie.

"I haven't seen her all day, and I've become worried. Normally I'd get up and go looking for her, but I'm afraid I've grown too weak."

"Oh no," said the short haired orange kitten,

Mickey.

"Don't worry," said Josie. "We'll find her for you."

"Oh, that would be wonderful," said Elder Stan. "Thank you, kittens. I think I'm going to try and rest my eyes a bit now."

The four kittens stepped outside, where they discussed their plan to find Zoe.

"Do you guys think Mrs. Zoe is okay?" asked Daisy. "I wonder where she could be."

"We'll find her, no worries," Josie insisted.

"You sure sound confident," said Daisy.

"I think we should split up," suggested Minnie. "That way we can cover more ground and hopefully find her faster."

"Good idea," said Mickey, and the other cats agreed as well.

"But we should try not to stir up a panic," Minnie added, glancing over at Josie. "So keep that in mind as we ask around for her."

"Okay, okay," said Josie.

* * *

Josie and Daisy split off then and ventured into town to look for Zoe,

Minnie and Mickey stuck together and

decided to head for home first.

"Hi, Mom," Minnie said as she and Mickey entered their home.

"Hi you two," said their mother, Mia, who Minnie looked like a miniature version of. "Where are your sisters at?"

"Oh, they're off playing Ninja Kitties," said Minnie.

"And you didn't want to play with them?" asked Mia.

"Not right now," said Minnie. "Hey Mom, you haven't seen Mrs. Zoe today, have you?"

"Hmm," Mia thought for a moment. "No, I don't think that I have. She wasn't home with Elder Stan?"

"She wasn't," said Mickey.

"Well that's odd," said Mia. "Well, maybe you can ask Miss Chloe. They're such good friends, maybe Zoe just needed to see a friend."

"Ooh, good idea," said Mickey. "Thanks, Mom."

The door opened again then, and in stepped a big orange cat who Mickey looked like a miniature version of (though there was no relation).

"Hello, Tom," Mia said.

"Hello, Mia. Hi kittens," said Tom.

"Hi, Mr. Tom," both Minnie and Mickey said together.

"What're you two doing home so early? I thought you'd be out playing with your sisters."

"Mr. Tom," said Mickey, "you haven't seen Mrs. Zoe today, have you?"

"Can't say that I have," said Tom. "Why, did you need her for something?"

"Nope!" said Minnie, who quickly quieted Mickey before he could utter another word. "We were just curious. We're off to see Miss Chloe now. Goodbye, Tom. Goodbye, Mom."

"Goodbye, kittens. Stay out of trouble," Mia said, and the two stepped back outside.

As they were closing the door behind them, they could overhear Tom asking, "What was that all about?"

"Whew, that was close," said Minnie, after fully shutting the door. "Come on, Mickey, let's go see Miss Chloe and see if she's seen Mrs. Zoe."

"Right," said Mickey, and the two left for Chloe's home.

* * *

Upon arrival, Minnie knocked on the door, and Chloe checked to see who was there.

"Oh, hello, kittens," said the elderly fluffy gray cat Chloe.

"Hi, Miss Chloe," both Minnie and Mickey said together.

"What brings you two here?"

"We were just wondering if you've seen Mrs. Zoe today," said Minnie.

"Oh, I am sorry, but I can not say that I have," said Chloe. "Why, is something the matter?"

"Oh no, we were just curious," said Minnie.

"I see," said Chloe. "Well, perhaps she is out running errands. Elder Stan is not feeling too well, so she may have stepped out to gather ingredients to cook him some chicken soup."

"That might be," said Minnie.

"But Josie and Daisy are already in town looking for her," said Mickey, to which Minnie promptly shushed him.

"I see," said Chloe. "Then perhaps you might consider checking with the village guardians to see if she might have stepped out of the village for a bit."

"That's a good idea," said Minnie. "Thank you, Miss Chloe."

"Good luck," said Chloe, "and let me know when you find her."

"We will," said Minnie.

*** * * *

Next the two kittens made their way to the village gates. They looked around for the village guardians, but there was no one in sight.

"Huh, there's nobody here," said Mickey. "That's strange."

"Looking for someone?" they heard a voice call out to them.

The two looked around, but they still couldn't see anyone.

"Who was that?" asked Mickey. "Was that you, Minnie?"

"Don't be silly," said Minnie.

"Up here," they heard the voice say again, and the two looked up to find a black calico cat watching them from high up in a tree.

"Oh, hello, Pepper," said Mickey.

"Hello, kittens," said Pepper. "Were you two looking for someone?"

"Yes, we were wondering if you might have seen Mrs. Zoe come this way," said Minnie.

"Hmm, I can't say that I have," said Pepper. "How about you, Honey?"

A white calico cat, Honey, popped her head up from behind a branch. She hissed in response to Pepper's question, which sent the kittens' fur standing on end.

"Sorry, kittens," said Pepper.

"That's okay," said Minnie. "Thank you."

Minnie and Mickey turned to head back into town, when Mickey asked, "Well now what, Minnie?"

"Maybe we should regroup with Josie and Daisy, and see if they've found anything," said Minnie.

"Right," said Mickey.

* * *

Minnie and Mickey headed back to Elder Stan's home, when they saw Josie and Daisy approaching from the opposite end.

"Did you guys have any luck?" asked Josie.

"No," said Minnie.

"Yeah, same on our end," said Josie.

"So now what?" asked Daisy.

"Hmm, I don't know," said Minnie.

"I do!" said Josie. She then pulled out a ninja headband, and she wrapped it around her head. "We put our training to the test and seek her out like the Ninja Kitties we are!"

"Yeah!" said Daisy, and she wrapped a ninja headband around her head as well.

"Well, what do you think, Minnie?" asked Mickey.

With a sigh, she responded, "Okay, let's do it." Both she and Mickey wrapped ninja headbands around their heads, and Minnie asked, "Where to first?"

"Well, we've already checked all over the village, so let's see if she's somewhere on the outskirts," Josie suggested.

"To the Twin Tree then?" asked Minnie.

"That's exactly what I was thinking," said Josie.

* * *

The four kittens then set out for the Twin Tree. They rushed past it, heading for the village outskirts, but as they passed the tree, something caught Minnie's eye, and she stopped in her tracks.

"Wait," Minnie said.

The other three stopped and turned to look back at the Twin Tree. There they found the one-legged cat Zoe sitting on the grass, hiding behind the tree with her head on her knee.

"Oh, well that was easy," said Daisy.

"Mrs. Zoe, is that you?" asked Minnie.

Zoe lifted her head, then quickly wiped tears

from her eyes.

"Prr, oh, kittens," said Zoe. "What brings you all out here?"

"We were looking for you, Mrs. Zoe," said Mickey.

"Prr, oh no, I hope I didn't worry you."

"Heh, not at all!" boasted Josie.

"*But*," Minnie interjected, "Elder Stan *is* worried about you."

"Prr, oh my Stan, I can't bear to see him like this. It just breaks my heart."

The four kittens then stepped up next to Zoe.

"But Elder Stan needs you now, Mrs. Zoe," said Minnie.

"And he needs you to be strong for him," said Josie.

"And besides," said Mickey, "you'll regret it if you don't give yourself the chance to say goodbye."

The other kittens lowered their heads.

"Prr, oh my, you silly kittens sure have grown," said Zoe with a proud smile. "Okay, would you all be so kind as to help an old cat see to her husband?"

"Of course," said Minnie, handing Zoe her crutch as Daisy aided her up to her foot. Then the kittens helped Zoe back to her home.

* * *

Upon arrival, the kittens escorted Zoe inside her home. Zoe opened the bedroom door, and the kittens watched from outside the room as Zoe hopped over to Elder Stan's bedside.

Stan slowly opened his eyes, and they appeared to glimmer at the sight of his wife.

"Zoe, is that you?" Stan asked.

"It's me, Stan. I'm here," Zoe said with a sad smile, holding Stan's hand in hers.

Stan was relieved to see his beloved by his side, and the four kittens smiled from the doorway, shutting the door on another successful Ninja Kitties mission.

* * *

Some days later, Elder Stan sadly passed away.

The villagers had all gathered together to attend his funeral, including Minnie and Mickey, Josie and Daisy, Mia and Tom, Pepper and Honey, Miss Chloe, and Elder Stan's wife Zoe, and many others. They looked upon Elder Stan's casket as it was being lowered into the ground, wearing solemn faces and tears in their eyes.

When Zoe started to cry, Mickey placed a comforting palm on the elderly cat's shoulder.

Minnie then stepped up to speak.

"Elder Stan was this village's rock," said Minnie. "He helped raise all of us, and he was always calm and comforting. He was a great leader who lead by example. I just hope that we can continue to live by his example. And I hope we can make him proud as we carry his legacy forward with us."

Minnie glanced over to her siblings, and they all returned a sorrowful smile, while Zoe and the other adults looked up proudly at her.

"Goodbye, Elder Stan. You'll live on in our hearts."

VITIATE

Vitiate was a mischievous cat. A scraggly haired brown tabby, his owner would oftentimes leave their apartment door open for him to slip outside for some freedom and mayhem. He'd wander around the complex parking lot, where none of the other neighborhood cats dared to mess with him, because Vitiate had a peculiar power. He had the ability to shoot lightning bolts from his paws, and he relished this power for the selfish advantage it gave him.

The other cats in the complex all feared him. He'd raise his paw to them and strike out his bolts of lightning right in front of them, then laugh as they sprang in the air and dash off in fear. Sometimes he'd even carelessly shock them in his attempt to frighten, or damage nearby property in his reckless efforts. Other times he'd wander into the woods behind the complex and use his lightning to strike down a bird with a chuckle. Or worse yet, he might strike his lightning at another cat and steal their bird for his own, to which he would return as a gift to his owner with menacing elation, taking the credit all for himself.

Then one day, in a garden out back, Vitiate caught sight of a new cat he hadn't seen in the complex before. Snickering to himself, he slunk out of sight in the bushes and stalked the new cat. He charged up his lightning with intent to catch the cat off guard, but it was Vitiate who was caught off guard as the cat knowingly snapped its head in his direction.

"I see you there," the cat spoke, and then he stood up on his hind legs. "Your tricks won't have the same effect on me as they do your other victims. Just try it," the cat challenged.

Vitiate hopped out of the bushes, and with a snarl, he sent a bolt of lightning from his paw right at the cat. With a swipe, however, the new cat was able to deflect the attack with ease.

"I hail from the Realm of Spirits," the cat continued, "and your unique abilities caught my attention. However, I'm sad to see the way that you've chosen to use these special powers of yours. You're a wild cat, so it's not entirely your fault, but under my tutelage, you can become domesticated and disciplined, and learn how to use your powers for good."

Vitiate growled as the cat spoke, his fur standing on end.

"But I leave that choice up to you," the cat continued. "Either follow this new path that I present to you, under my guidance or of your own volition, or I will be forced to put an end to your wicked ways myself, before you take things too far."

Vitiate hissed in response, and he shot another bolt of lightning out to the cat. This time, rather than deflect, the cat merely evaded the lightning, allowing it to strike at the dirt behind him as he stood his ground unruffled.

"I've trained ninja cats during my time," the cat explained, "so your attacks won't work against me like they might against just any old cat."

With a growl, Vitiate struck another bolt of lightning, but this time the cat caught it. He twirled the lightning in his paw, before turning it back to Vitiate and striking him with his own attack. In a spark, Vitiate was sent sailing from the blow, and whined as he fell hard to the ground.

"I'll give you one last chance," the cat spoke, now approaching the downed villain. "Either take my offer, or you'll leave me with no choice but to end this now."

The cat extended his paw down to Vitiate.

Through pained eyes, Vitiate glared up at the paw, then into the cat's eyes. He growled under his breath, then he raised up his own paw. But then he ceased growling, and rather than continue the fight, Vitiate reluctantly placed his paw into the other cat's.

"That's more like it," the cat said, and he helped Vitiate back onto his feet. "You have potential. And under my guidance, you can learn how to truly harness your powers. However, should you choose to go against our agreement, I will not waver in striking you down again. Do you understand?"

Vitiate meowed in agreement, then asked the cat what he should call him.

"You may refer to me as Master," the cat said. When Vitiate responded that he already had a master, the cat reiterated his stance. "No, what you have right now is an *owner*. But from here on out, *I* am your master."

Vitiate meowed his acknowledgment, and the master cat nodded in approval.

"Good, then we'll begin our training immediately," said the master cat.

"Meow," said Vitiate back.

* * *

After months of rigorous training, the master cat was willing to allow Vitiate to roam the complex alone, curious how he might carry himself. Vitiate walked with his head up straight, and he minded his own business as he wandered about. When the neighborhood cats caught sight of him, they initially fled in fear. But they were surprised to see him leave them be, and watched in confusion as he continued on his way without an inkling of his formerly wild nature.

When he crossed paths with his master on his way back home, he stopped and turned. The master cat nodded back in approval, and Vitiate smiled at the recognition.

"RROOWWRR!!"

The two cats heard the crying wail of another cat nearby, coming from the garden out back. Quickly they rushed to the source of the cries, and there they found the neighborhood cat trapped with its back to the wall, as a large dog growled at it threateningly. The cat hissed, its fur standing up straight, but there was nowhere for it to go, lest the dog snatch it in its attempt to escape.

Vitiate turned to his master. His master gave him a nod, and Vitiate nodded back. He then conjured up his lightning powers, and he let out a viscous meow, catching the dog's attention. The dog turned to Vitiate, barking from the activity of the lightning, when Vitiate tossed out his bolt, striking the ground with controlled precision just in front of the dog. The dog yelped in fear and ran away, as did the frightened cat. But before running off too far, the cat stopped and turned to Vitiate, and it nodded its head in thanks before rushing off to safety.

The master cat placed a proud paw on Vitiate's back. "You did well," he said, "and you've come so far since we first met."

Vitiate turned to his master with pride. Curiously, he then asked if his master was willing to share his real name with him just yet.

"Heh," the master cat said, with a smirk and a wink. "Not just yet. You may have come far, but you still have a lot left to learn. So for now, you may still refer to me as Master."

CORNHOLE

George and the other cats were still getting used to the new dog, Stella Bean. George was an orange cat, and he would watch the Jack Russell chihuahua Stella with care and curiosity, while the Siamese cat Penelope and his calico sister Jazmine chose to remain in hiding.

One day, while their parents were out of the house, Stella had found something under the couch, and was growling as she pulled it out. George saw that she had found a small bean bag under there, the type you might play a game of cornhole with, and she was shaking it around playfully in her mouth. Stella then released the bag, flinging it through the air. George's eyes widened as he saw the bag fall atop the fish tank, where it appeared to disappear. Stella barked up at the tank, then hopped on the couch, and jumped off onto the tank, where she also disappeared from sight.

George shook his head in disbelief. Then he, too, hopped up onto the couch. He leaned to see over the fish tank, and he made out what appeared to be some sort of hole on top. He hopped over onto the tank, and he saw that there was indeed a hole, the type you might see on a cornhole board. He looked around the room confused, when he heard Stella's barking coming from within the hole. Turning back down to it, he decided to peek his head in, but then he slipped and fell through the hole with a howling meow.

On the other side of the hole, George suddenly found himself outside, where he was falling through the air. He landed in a body of water, then quickly scrambled over to the nearby land. He shook himself dry, and saw that Stella was already on land shaking herself as well, and she had the bean bag back in her mouth.

"Honk."

The two turned, and they saw that they had caught the attention of a large goose, who looked none too pleased to see them. It honked at them again, then fluttered its wings hard as it flew at them to attack.

"Honk, honk!"

George and Stella quickly turned and sprinted into the woods and away from the shore. As George looked behind, he could see that the goose was still making chase, honking all the while.

114

Then as he looked forward, he saw as the bag fell from Stella's mouth, and it once again opened up a hole on the ground as it landed. Stella fell into the hole, then George skidded to a halt. He glanced at the hole, then back at the goose, and he quickly made his decision to follow Stella once more, hopping down into the hole after her.

He fell hard on the rocky ground. The area was dark, but George was still able to make out his surroundings, where he determined they had fallen into some sort of cave. He and Stella got back to their feet, when they heard a screeching sound from the distance. The sound grew louder as it approached them, and George could see that a colony of bats was flying right toward them.

George turned to Stella, then down to the bean bag. He then swatted at the bag and sent it flinging against the cave wall, where it once again opened another hole. George ushered Stella within, and he joined her through the hole just before the bats could make it to their location.

They landed safely on concrete ground, back outside in the sun. As George assessed their surroundings, it appeared that they had found themselves in an apartment complex parking lot. George sighed with relief, sure that they were finally safe. Stella leaned down to pick the bean bag back up into her mouth, but then a sudden bolt of lightning struck the ground right before them, and Stella dropped the bag in fright. A new hole opened up beneath them, and both George and Stella fell through it.

They landed on the floor of a Mexican restaurant, right in front of a mariachi band playing a festive song. One of the band members, a trumpeter, reached up to grab the bean bag that had landed on his head, then looked down at the cat and the dog with confusion. Stella barked, asking the man to toss the bag, but George looked unsure. The trumpeter shrugged, then tossed the bag to Stella, but it flew over her head and landed on the ground behind her, opening up another hole. Stella chased after the bag without an ounce of hesitation. With a sigh of annoyance, George jumped into the hole after Stella.

When they landed again, they were in an incredibly loud and dark room, with strobe lights flashing and people dancing all around them. George was in a panic, as they had appeared to fall right in the middle of a mosh pit during a heavy metal concert. Stella, however, was having a blast, and she barked happily as she danced along with the people.

One of the concertgoers noticed the bean bag

on the ground, and he kicked it up onto the air like a hacky sack. He kept it in the air, and kicked it over to a friend, who continued to keep the bag aloft. George's widened eyes remained glued to the bag with terror. As the second person kicked the bag to a third, George leaped up at it, swatting it down to the ground. When it hit the ground, another hole was opened. George bit on Stella's collar, dragging her away from the pit, then George dropped Stella into the hole before hopping in after her.

Once they fell through that hole, their descent was suddenly slowed down as they found themselves approaching the low gravitational pull of the moon's surface. Stella swam through the air towards the bean bag. She pawed it down to the ground, and it opened up yet another hole upon contact. Stella fell through first, and then George shortly after. All the while, a giant spider was watching them curiously from a safe distance.

George and Stella toppled hard onto the ground, and this time they found themselves in another dark room, but this one much quieter. Stella picked the bean bag back into her mouth, and as George's eyes adjusted, he realized that he recognized this room. It was the basement to their parent's house. At last, they had finally made it back home.

Not long after this realization, George could hear the front door opening upstairs, and his parents returning home. George and Stella rushed up the stairs, and they scratched at the door to be let in. Stella barked for her parents, and shortly, their mother greeted them at the door.

"Huh? How did you two get out here?" she asked, as she was bombarded by the cat and the dog who nearly took her off her feet. "Hi, George," she said, patting the cat's head. "Hi, Stella Bean," she said, and the dog hopped into her arms. George then saw as Jazmine and Penelope peeked at them curiously from around the corner.

"Hmm, what's this?" their mother asked, and she pulled the bean bag from Stella's mouth. She inspected it over, and then shrugged her shoulders, and tossed it back down the basement stairs. George and Stella shot their gaze at the bean bag, and they saw yet another hole appear on the floor of the basement just before their mother closed the door.

THE KITTYMETAL QUEEN

Whenever she was on stage in front of a crowd of adoring fans, the lovely young lady Blacky was hailed as a queen. Adorned in her grand attire, with her hair and face made up in ornate fashion, she carried herself in a striking and majestic manner. She was the lead vocalist of a metal band, Kittymetal, and was worshiped by her cult of fans. They obsessed over her, and obeyed her every command as she performed on the stage. It was like she held them in the palm of her hand, and they would bow to her every whim. They were cast under her spell, and looked up to her like she was true royalty.

* * *

There wouldn't be another show until the following night, so Blacky decided to go out and enjoy her day off in the best way she knew how. She was wearing a plain t-shirt and jeans, nothing too fancy. Her black hair was loose, and she didn't bother putting on any makeup. She took the subway into the city, and as she made her way around, she was ignored by everyone else around her.

Once in the city, she decided to make a trip to the grocery store. She wandered the aisles looking for snacks, but she wasn't familiar with this location, and so she got lost in the store. Eventually an employee noticed she looked lost, and asked her if he could help her find anything.

"No, I'm good, thanks," she replied.

"Okay, well let me know if you need any help."

As the employee was walking away, she had a sudden change of mind, and decided to ask him for help after all.

"*Actually,* I was looking for some chips and salsa," she told the employee.

"Right this way," he said, and walked her to where the chips were located in the store. "And just down there you'll find the salsa," he pointed down to the end of the aisle.

"Thank you," she said, and picked out her brand of chips. She placed them in her basket, then wandered over to the salsas. She found what she was looking for, when a container of guacamole caught her eye. She pondered for a moment, then decided to add the guac to her basket as well, and she made her way to the checkout.

As she was heading back to the subway, she passed by a coffee shop and decided to stop in. She ordered an ice coffee, and sweetened it with cream and sugar, just how she liked it. She sipped on her drink as she carried her bag of snacks onto the subway, and traveled back to her hotel room.

Once she made it back, she set up her food on the table. She then stepped out and knocked on the door of her bandmate's rooms, inviting them to join her. She and her friends all gathered in her room, and they had themselves a little salsa party.

The salsa had just the right kick, not too spicy, but not too mild either, and made for a very fulfilling snack. Blacky made sure to set aside the guacamole for later. The band members then all sat around eating their chips and telling stories, and sharing their hopes and dreams for the future.

"One day, I think I'd like to be a writer," Blacky confessed.

"But you're already a writer, aren't you?" asked her bandmate, Brownie.

"Well, yes, I write music, but I'd like to do more than that. I would like to write a book someday I think."

"I bet you have a wonderful story in you," said her other bandmade, Mama. "I'd love to read it."

After a while, Mama decided she wanted to spice up the party, and she pulled out her phone and put on some pop music. They all got out of their seats then, and they started dancing to the music, singing along and laughing and having a delightful time.

Then a puff of smoke erupted around each of the three ladies. When the smoke had cleared, the girls had disappeared, and three cats had replaced them in the hotel room. In Blacky's place was the fluffy black tabby, Josie. Where Brownie was now stood the fluffy brown cat, Daisy. And in Mama's spot was their short haired mama cat, Mia. But despite no longer disguised in their on-stage personas, the three cats continued to munch on chips and dance to the music well into the night.

* * *

The following day, the three cats ate the perfectly mixed batch of guacamole, which returned them to their human forms. Now back as Blacky, Brownie, and Mama, Josie and the others put on their lavish attire and made themselves up, and they went back on stage, where they once again performed in front of a crowd of devout fans. As with every night, they hailed Blacky as their queen, and seemingly elevated her to a goddess status in their eyes. However, deep down inside, Josie knew the truth, that she was really just a normal cat.

HEAVEN'S
COLLECTING CATS

Tom was always sort of a lazy cat. He had this aloof swagger to him as he walked, like he was in no real hurry, and nothing could get to him. But Daisy noticed when the manner in Tom's step changed. He still walked with no hurry, and he still couldn't be bothered. And yet, there was a frailty in his pace, which Daisy had recognized in other cats before.

Daisy recalled how recently the reclusive Honey had disappeared, and how not long before that, the always odd Chloe had disappeared as well. And both times, before they left for good, they had also grown frail, like Tom was doing now.

Daisy worried that she was about to lose another member of her cat family. And then one day, after Tom had wandered off to be by himself, it wasn't long before he, too, left their home for the last time.

After Tom disappeared, Daisy found herself sleeping in all of Tom's usual resting spots. She could still smell his scent left behind, and it brought tears to her eyes. She still had her sister Josie, and she still had her mother, Mia. But even so, Daisy missed the family she had lost.

It broke her heart to lose so many in her family in such quick succession. Daisy wondered where her family went. She wondered if she'd ever see them again. The more she wondered, the more she missed them. And the more she missed them, the more her heart ached.

But then one day, from the other room, Daisy heard Mom crying tears. So she quickly sprang up from Tom's old resting spot and rushed over to comfort Mom. She could see that Mom was in pain, too, and that only broke Daisy's heart even further.

Eventually, Daisy secluded herself in sadness, and she, too, began to grow frail. She had lost her appetite, and as she cried over her lost family, she closed her eyes for the last time...

* * *

... When Daisy reopened her eyes, she was met with a bright, cloudy sight. She had to shield herself from the shining light. But once her eyes adjusted, she made out figures up ahead, standing just within a glorious gate. She then realized those figures were other cats, and they weren't just any cats, but they were *her* cats. And her tears of sadness turned to tears of joy at the sight of her long lost family.

Tom waved her over first, no longer looking frail, and she waltzed up to him with glee. But as she looked past him, she saw both Honey and Chloe were there, too. And not just them, but her other family members who had disappeared long before, including Pepper, and Zoe, and Stan. Even her brother Mickey was there, who she hadn't seen since they were both still kittens. Daisy was overwhelmed with happiness at the sight of them all.

But that moment of happiness was fleeting, and Daisy worried that she had made Mom sad again. Tom reassured her though that of course Mom was sad, but that she had given her so many wonderful memories to look back on, and that those memories would make Mom happy again. And besides, she still had Josie and Mia to cheer her up.

Daisy then looked behind her, only just then realizing that neither Josie nor Mia had come with her. But Tom got her attention, and he once again assured her that it would be okay. In due time, they would reunite with everyone else they loved. But hopefully that time wouldn't come for a long time from now, and he winked.

Tom then ushered Daisy through the gates, telling her to come on, they've all been waiting, and it's been too long since she's been acquainted with her old family. And as they stepped into the shining light, he told her that they had all decided that this was where they were going to collect together, right here in heaven.

I would like to thank everyone who directly contributed to the creation of this book, including Christine Celenski, Kristen Moran, M.H. Smith, Tim Widdop, and my Uncle Bob and Aunt Laurie.

And I would especially like to thank my mom, without whom this book would not have been possible.

Chris Widdop grew up with his cat, Velcro. And together, the two would constantly escape into the fantasy world that was their vivid imaginations, where they took part in many adventures. And now, Chris wants nothing more than to share those adventures with the world.

www.ingramcontent.com/pod-product-compliance
Lightning Source LLC
Chambersburg PA
CBHW072028170626
46811CB00008B/2990